Chicken Little
A Folk & Fairy Tale Reader

retold by Liza Charlesworth
illustrated by Ian Smith

ISBN 978-0-545-76727-9

12 11 10   17 18 19

Printed in the U.S.A.   40
First printing, September 2014

Designed by Maria Mercado

SCHOLASTIC INC.

Look at Chicken Little.
He got hit on the head.
Bop!

"The sky is falling!" he said.
"I must tell the king."
So off he went.

Chicken Little saw a duck.
"The sky is falling!" he said.

"Oh, no!" said the duck.
"We must tell the king."
So off they went.

They saw a turkey.
"The sky is falling!" said Chicken Little.

"Oh, no!" said the turkey.
"We must tell the king."
So off they went.

They saw a fox.
"The sky is falling!" said Chicken Little.

"Oh, no!" said the fox.
"Come in my cave to be safe."

They went in the cave.
But the fox was hungry.

He tried to eat them up.
"Oh, no!" said Chicken Little.

They ran away from the fox.

Then they went to see the king.
"The sky is falling!" said Chicken Little.

"Oh, no!" said the king.
"Take this."

Look at Chicken Little.
The sky never hurt him again.
Bop!

Comprehension Boosters

1. Why did Chicken Little think the sky was falling?

2. How did the king help Chicken Little?

3. Chicken Little was silly. Use three more words to describe him.